Name:

Doctor:

First published 2007 by Walker Books Ltd
87 Vauxhall Walk, London SE11 5HJ

This edition published 2008

10 9

© 2007 Lucy Cousins
Lucy Cousins font © 2007 Lucy Cousins

The author/illustrator has asserted her moral rights

"Maisy" audio visual series produced by King Rollo Films Ltd
for Universal Pictures International Visual Programming

Maisy™. Maisy is a registered trademark of Walker Books Ltd, London

Printed in China

British Library Cataloguing in Publication Data:
a catalogue record for this book is
available from the British Library

ISBN 978-1-4063-1326-0

www.walker.co.uk

Maisy
Goes to Hospital

Lucy Cousins

WALKER BOOKS
AND SUBSIDIARIES
LONDON • BOSTON • SYDNEY • AUCKLAND

One day Maisy
was bouncing on
her trampoline.
She bounced
very high.

Oh, no!
Maisy fell.
She hurt her leg.

Poor Maisy!

Charley went with
Maisy to the hospital.

Maisy had never been to hospital before.

"You need to have an X-ray," Doctor Duck told Maisy.

The X-ray showed that Maisy had broken her leg.

Doctor Duck put a plaster cast on Maisy's leg.

Nurse Comfort put
Maisy to bed in
the children's ward.

Maisy's leg was raised
in a special lift.

It felt strange being away from home. Maisy missed her friends.

"Hello, my name's Dotty," said the patient in the opposite bed.

"I'm Maisy."
Maisy and Dotty
swapped toys.

The next morning during visiting hours, Tallulah and Cyril arrived.

Maisy shared her balloons and cakes with Dotty.

When it was time to go, Tallulah signed Maisy's plaster cast.

"You can go home now, Maisy," said Doctor Duck. "But no trampolining yet! Come back in a few weeks to have the cast taken off."

Before Maisy left,
Nurse Comfort showed
her how to walk
using crutches.

Charley arrived to take Maisy home. "Goodbye, Dotty," Maisy said to her new friend.

"Get well soon!"